GW00854048

STARTING POINT
SCIENCE

VOLUME 4

CONTENTS

WHY DO PEOPLE EAT?

Kate Needham

Designed by Lindy Dark and Non Figg

Illustrated by Annabel Spenceley and Kuo Kang Chen

Consultants: Dr Frank Slattery and Valerie Micheau

CONTENTS

Why do you need food?

Your body is like a big machine that is always working. Even when you are asleep your heart is beating, your lungs are breathing and your brain is working. Food is the fuel which keeps all these things going. Without it you would slow down and eventually grind to a halt.

A bar of chocolate gives you enough energy to walk for an hour.

People need food just as cars need petrol.

An apple gives you enough energy to cycle for six minutes.

Growing big and strong

People sometimes say you have to eat things to grow big and strong. This is true because your whole body is made from good things in the food you eat.

Until you are about 18 your body is growing all the time.

Measure yourself each month to see how quickly you grow.

Sometimes when you haven't eaten you feel weak. This is because your body is running out of energy.

Children who don't get enough food stop growing. They become thin and weak and fall ill more easily.

Too much

If you eat more food than your body needs you store it as fat. This makes you heavy and slows you down.

Some people want to be big and heavy so they overeat on purpose. For example Japanese sumo wrestlers need to be heavy to fight.

Sumo wrestlers look like this.

On the mend

The good things in the food you eat help your body make repairs if it gets damaged. They also help you get better when you are ill.

When you cut yourself, the food you eat helps your body mend quickly.

Water

Water is what keeps your body moist and makes your blood flow around. Without it your body would dry out and stop working.

You can last several weeks without food but only a few days without water.

Loading and unloading bread from an oven is hot, thirsty work.

Shipwrecked sailors more often die of thirst than hunger, since they can't drink seawater.

People who work in hot places, such as a baker, need to drink more because they lose water when they sweat.

What is food made of?

Everything you eat is made up of lots of different things called nutrients. These are the good things that keep your body going. Proteins, fats and carbohydrates are all nutrients. Each one helps your body do a special job.

Protein

Proteins are like building blocks. Your body uses them to grow and repair itself. Different kinds of proteins help build up each part of your body.

Pregnant women need extra protein to help their baby grow.

A mother's milk has special proteins in it.

Proteins build up muscles and make your hair grow.

Teenagers use up lots of proteins because they are growing fast.

Meat, eggs, fish and cheese have lots of protein.

4

Carbohydrate

Carbohydrates give you energy. You need energy for everything you do such as running around, talking, thinking, even reading this book.

You get lots of energy from sweet things but it doesn't last very long. The energy you get from pasta, cereal or bread is better because it lasts longer.

Climbers often carry a bar of chocolate in case they need extra energy in an emergency.

Sporty people need carbohydrate for extra energy.

Bread, cereal, pasta and cakes have lots of carbohydrate.

Fat

Fat also gives you energy but unless your body needs it right away, it is stored in a layer around your body. This acts like an extra piece of clothing helping to keep you warm and protect you.

Fat stored on your bottom makes it more comfortable to sit on, like a little cushion.

Butter, margarine and oil are almost all fat.

What else is in food?

The food you eat also has tiny amounts of nutrients called vitamins and minerals which you need.

What do vitamins do?

Vitamins are like little workers which help other nutrients to do their jobs. There are about 20 different kinds. Most are named after letters of the alphabet.

The chart opposite shows what some vitamins do and where you find them.

A

Vitamin A helps you see in the dark.

You find it in egg yolks, liver, full fat milk and carrots.

B

There are lots of kinds of B vitamins, each with a different job.

Cereals, dairy products and meat have B vitamins.

C

Vitamin C is good for health and body repairs.

You find it in fresh fruit and vegetables.

D

Vitamin D helps make your bones and teeth strong.

You get it from eggs, fish and butter.

Sailors used to get scurvy – a disease which stops wounds from healing. This is because they were at sea for months without any fresh vegetables or fruit and so no vitamin C.

Your body can make vitamin D itself using sunlight. People who live in less sunny countries need extra vitamin D from their food.

What are minerals?

Minerals are nutrients that plants get from soil and pass on to you. You need about 15 different ones such as salt, calcium and iron.

Water has lots of minerals in it.

Liver, meat and spinach have tiny amounts of iron in them which you need for your blood.

Milk, cheese and yogurt have calcium in them which makes your teeth and bones strong.

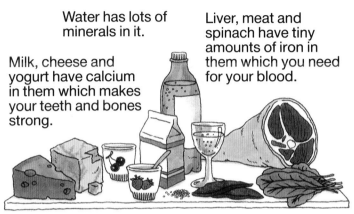

What is fibre?

Fibre is the tough bit of food that you don't digest. It helps carry food through you and takes waste out the other end.

Brown bread, cereals and vegetables have lots of fibre.

If you don't eat enough fibre you get constipated – this is when you can't go to the toilet for ages.

What do you eat?

Write down everything you ate and drank in your last main meal. Then see if you can find out which nutrients each thing had. Use the last two pages for help.

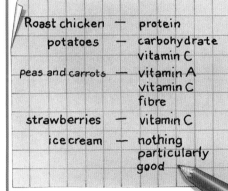

Roast chicken	—	protein
potatoes	—	carbohydrate vitamin C
peas and carrots	—	vitamin A vitamin C fibre
strawberries	—	vitamin C
ice cream	—	nothing particularly good

How many good things did you eat? Were there any you didn't get any of? Some things you eat, such as ice cream, may not have anything particularly good in them, see page 16.

7

Where does food go to?

When you eat, your food starts a long journey through your body which takes about three days. It travels through a tube called the alimentary canal which starts at your mouth and finishes at your bottom.

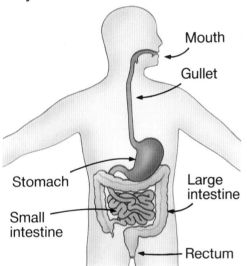

Mouth

Gullet

Stomach

Small intestine

Large intestine

Rectum

On the way, different parts of your body work on the food and add juices with chemicals in them. This breaks food into microscopically small pieces that can go into your blood. This journey is called digestion.

Food's journey

The road in this picture is like the alimentary canal, and the men show what happens to your food.

Your mouth

These men are like your teeth, cutting food into tiny pieces.

The water is like saliva. It makes food soft and mushy.

Your tongue rolls the food into a ball and pushes it into your gullet, like these men with brooms.

Your gullet

Then you swallow, and food is carried off from your mouth to continue its journey.

8

How long to chew?

The smaller food gets in your mouth, the easier it is for your stomach to work on. Tough meat or food with lots of fibre needs more chewing.

Eat a mouthful of apple. Then eat one of cheese.

See how many times you chew each one before you swallow .

What makes you choke?

Your gullet is next to your windpipe (the pipe you breath through). When you swallow, your windpipe closes to stop food from going into it.

If it doesn't close in time your food might go down the wrong way. This makes you choke which usually sends the food back up.

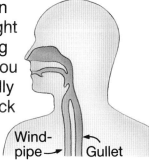

Wind-
pipe→ Gullet

Your stomach

To your intestines

In your body, it goes off down a tube called your gullet. This delivers food to your stomach by squeezing it along.

Your stomach is like a big mixing machine. It churns your food up until it is like soup.

Your stomach stretches to hold enough food to last you several hours. Turn the page to see what happens in the intestines, where food is pushed to next.

Good things and waste

After about three hours, the soupy mixture in your stomach moves on to your intestines. There, all the good things in food are taken into the blood. The way it happens is called absorption. Waste moves on to leave your body. This is the longest part of food's journey.

How goodness is absorbed

The walls of your small intestine are so thin that the nutrients in your food can pass through them.

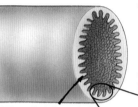

The nutrients go into your blood and are carried around your body.

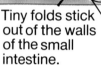

Tiny folds stick out of the walls of the small intestine.

Blood flows all around the folds, ready to carry off nutrients.

goodness

waste

STAY

Your small intestine

First the food arrives in your small intestine. This isn't really small at all, as it's a long tube all curled up.

As the soupy mixture passes through it, more juices are added. Then nutrients are absorbed into your blood (the man's sign tells them to stay). The rest goes into your large intestine (the man's sign tells them they must go).

Your large intestine

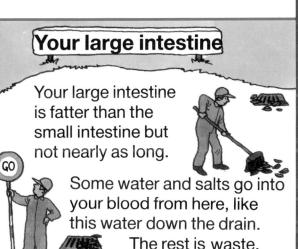

Your large intestine is fatter than the small intestine but not nearly as long.

Some water and salts go into your blood from here, like this water down the drain. The rest is waste.

Getting rid of waste

Waste from your large intestine is solid. It goes into your rectum and is pushed out through your bottom when you go to the toilet.

Waste water is turned into urine (wee) in your kidneys. It is stored in your bladder until you go to the toilet.

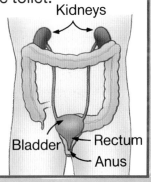

Kidneys

Bladder — Rectum

Anus

What makes you burp?

When you eat you often swallow air with your food. Sometimes your body sends the air back up through your mouth. This is a burp.

BURP!

Eating too fast makes you swallow lots of air and so you may burp.

Food poisoning

If you eat food that is bad, your body tries to get rid of it quickly.

Your stomach muscles may push it back up your gullet. This is when you are sick.

It may rush through you and come out the other end as diarrhoea.

11

Keeping food fresh

Your food is also food for tiny living things called microbes. These can make fresh food go bad after a few days. If you want food to keep you have to stop microbes from getting at it first. They like moisture, warmth and air, so food kept in cold, dry places with no air lasts longer.

No air

Today, lots of food is vacuum-packed. This is when all the air is sucked out of the packet. Bottles and cans have no air either. Can you hear air rushing back in when you open them?

VACUUM-PACKED PEANUTS

Keeping food cold

Cooling food slows microbes down; freezing it stops them altogether. Today, food can be kept in refrigerators or freezers until it is needed.

Cold cellars have been used to keep food for centuries.

The cold does not kill microbes, so you still have to eat food quickly when you defrost it.

Drying food

Drying food gets rid of all the moisture so microbes can't multiply.

Grapes are dried to make raisins, sultanas and currants.

Today, food can be freeze-dried. This is when it is frozen and dried at the same time to get rid of moisture. You add water when you eat it.

Astronauts use freeze-dried food as it's light and takes little room.

Heating food up

Cooking, sterilization and pasteurization are all ways of killing microbes by heat.

Sterilized food is heated to a very high temperature to kill all the microbes. It lasts a long time.

Sugar in jam

Vinegar in pickles

Salt in bacon

Food in cans and bottles is sterilized.

Preservatives: Benzoic acid (E210)

Preservatives

Preservatives are chemicals that make food last. Natural ones like sugar, vinegar and salt, have been used for centuries.

Look at labels on cans to see what other chemicals are used as preservatives today.

Pasteurized milk is heated enough to kill dangerous microbes. It lasts a few days.

Before pasteurization, cows were led around towns and milked on the doorstep.

Food you store loses some nutrients, particularly vitamins, so it is better to eat fresh food.

Food from far away

These days food can be kept fresh for so long that shops have exotic fruits from all over the world. They travel in specially refrigerated ships.

Next time you go to a supermarket, see if it says where the fruit comes from on the shelves.

Pineapple

Mangoes

Banana   Passion fruit
   Lychees

13

What makes you hungry?

When your body needs food, it sends a message to your brain to say so. Then you look around to find something to eat.

Sometimes, when you see or smell food you like, it can make you feel hungry even though your body doesn't need food.

Nose smells food

Eyes see food

The smell of food tells you if it is good or bad and if you like it or not.

Even thinking about food can make you feel hungry.

Stomach is empty

What makes your mouth water?

When you see or smell food you like, your body gets ready to eat. You may feel water in your mouth. This is saliva, the juice your mouth makes to help mix your food.

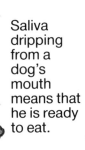

Saliva dripping from a dog's mouth means that he is ready to eat.

Tummy rumbles

Sometimes, when your stomach is getting ready for food, it makes a rumbling noise. The sound you can hear is air and digestive juices being pushed around inside.

Tasting food

You can tell what food you do and don't like by the taste of it. Your tongue is what you mainly use to taste food. It is covered with lots of tiny bumps called taste buds.

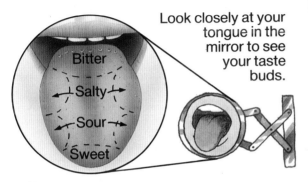

Look closely at your tongue in the mirror to see your taste buds.

There are four types of taste buds. Each tells a different kind of taste: salty, sweet, sour and bitter. They are on different parts of your tongue.

The smell of things helps you taste them as well. Try holding your nose when you eat. Can you taste your food?

Try this

Dip your finger in some salt. Put it on the tip of your tongue, then on the back and finally on the side. Which part can you taste it on most?

Do the same with sugar, lemon juice and coffee. Can you tell which kind of taste they are?

See if you can fill in a chart like the one below.

Food	Part of tongue	Taste
Salt	Back of side	
Sugar		sweet
Lemon		
Coffee		

Professional tasters

Some people can tell different tastes more easily than others. They may become professional wine- or tea-tasters.

Food that's bad for you

If you only ate your favourite food, your body wouldn't get all the good things it needs.

Some foods have very little goodness and can be bad for you if you eat too much of them.

Sweet things

Sugar is what makes things sweet. It is a carbohydrate so it gives you energy, but too much of it makes you fat. It also makes your teeth rot.

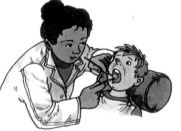

The more sweet things you eat, the more fillings you are likely to have at the dentist's.

Fatty food

Food that is fried, such as a burger, has lots of extra fat. It makes you feel full so you may not eat other things that are good for you.

Having extra fat is like carrying heavy bags. Your body and heart have to work harder to carry the weight.

What is junk food?

Food that has mostly bad things and very few good things in it is called junk food.

Sweets and fizzy drinks are nearly all sugar.

Ice creams, milk shakes and biscuits are mostly fat and sugar.

Fast food is often fried and so has extra fat.

16

What is a food allergy?

Some people feel bad every time they eat a certain kind of food. They may get a headache or a rash or be sick. This is called a food allergy.

One person's favourite food can make another person feel really ill.

Quite a lot of people are allergic to fish, eggs, strawberries or shellfish.

Special problems with food

Some people's bodies can't store sugar so they can only eat a little of it. Some need injections to help their body use sugar properly. This problem is called diabetes.

Some chocolate is made without sugar so that people with diabetes can enjoy it, too.

Other people's bodies don't like gluten – a protein in wheat. They can't eat things with wheat or wheat flour in them. This problem is called coeliac disease.

Can you guess which things in this picture have wheat in them? The answer is at the bottom of page 18.

Religion

Some people don't eat certain kinds of food because their religion says they shouldn't. Muslims and Jews don't eat pork, for example.

Where does food come from?

Almost everything you eat comes from a living thing: either a plant or an animal.

Bread and cereals come from corn.

Beef, cheese and milk come from cows.

Plants make their own food, using energy from the sun. Animals eat plants or other animals. So do people. The way one thing eats another is called a food chain.

Energy from the sun.

You get energy from cow's milk.

Energy goes from the grass to the cow.

In this picture, do you know where all the picnic food comes from? Can you find out what the food chain of the egg is? Turn to the bottom of page 20 for the answer.

Answer from page 17: All of them.

People who don't eat meat

People who choose not to eat any meat are called vegetarians. Some don't like the taste of meat. Others don't like to kill animals and think the way they are kept is cruel.

Some people don't eat anything at all that comes from animals. They are called vegans.

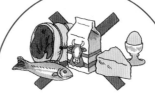

Vegans don't eat meat, fish, milk, eggs and cheese.

Vegetarians don't eat meat. Some don't eat fish.

Most people get most of the protein they need from meat, though there is some in plants. Vegetarians and vegans must take care to get enough protein.

How are animals kept?

For most farmers it is more important to produce lots of food cheaply, than it is to give an animal a nice life. This is because people usually buy cheaper food.

Hens that run around the farm are called free-range hens.

For example, hens usually stop laying eggs at night. But if they are kept in warm cages with the lights on, they lay for longer.

Hens kept in cages are called battery hens. They can lay about 270 eggs a year.

A free-range hen may only lay 80 eggs a year, so its eggs are more expensive.

Is there enough food?

If all the food in the world was spread evenly among all the people, everyone would have enough to eat. But it isn't like that.

In rich parts of the world like Europe, North America and Australia, most people get plenty to eat. Some eat too much.

Families in rich countries tend to be smaller so there are fewer people to share the food.

In poor parts of the world like Africa, South East Asia and South America people have a lot less to eat. Many don't get enough.

Families in these countries tend to be larger so there are more mouths to feed.

Other problems in poor countries

Without rain you cannot grow things. Some African countries have had no rain for several years and their farmland is now desert.

If there is a war, land for growing food may be destroyed. Often food from other countries can't get through to help feed people.

Answer from page 18: egg – chicken – corn.

What is malnutrition?

Malnutrition is when people don't get enough of the right nutrients. This means they catch diseases more easily.

In many poor countries people don't get enough protein. Children especially need protein to grow. Most protein comes from animals. They are expensive to keep so many people can't afford them.

What is a famine?

A famine is when there is so little food that people die. Often they die of diseases caused by malnutrition.

Who helps?

There are organizations in rich countries which send some food and help to places where there is famine.

Future food

If the population of the whole world keeps growing there won't be enough food for everyone, particularly meat, fish and eggs.

So scientists are busy searching for new kinds of food, especially plants with lots of protein.

Soya is a plant from China which has lots of protein. It can be made to look and taste like other food.

Some seaweeds are rich in protein. It grows all over the world but it is only eaten in a few countries, such as Japan, so far.

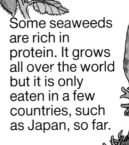

Around the world

People in different countries eat different things. This is because each part of the world has different plants and animals. This map shows you three main crops that grow in different parts of the world.

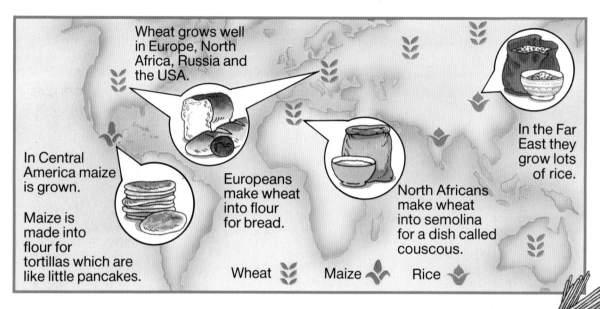

Wheat grows well in Europe, North Africa, Russia and the USA.

In Central America maize is grown.

Maize is made into flour for tortillas which are like little pancakes.

Europeans make wheat into flour for bread.

North Africans make wheat into semolina for a dish called couscous.

In the Far East they grow lots of rice.

Wheat 🌾 Maize 🌽 Rice 🌾

Food that has travelled

Lots of the food we eat every day was first found in distant countries by explorers.

Potatoes were discovered by the Spanish in South America in the 16th century.

Turkeys were also found by the Spanish, in Mexico.

Spices like cloves, pepper and cinnamon were carried back from the East in the Middle Ages.

Pasta was found in the Far East by the famous Italian explorer Marco Polo.

Unusual food

People in other countries eat all sorts of things that you may never have tried.

In some parts of the world people eat insects which have lots of protein in them.

On Chinese stalls like this one you can buy beetles, bats, snakes or even so-called 100 year-old eggs.

Insects are common food in many parts of Africa.

Ants are eaten in Columbia.

Grasshoppers are cooked and eaten in Mexico.

Ways to eat

In Western countries most people eat with a knife and fork.

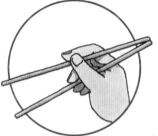

In countries in the Far East people use two wooden sticks called chopsticks.

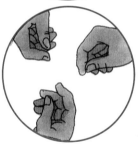

In India everyone eats from the same dish with one hand only, always the right hand.

Holidays abroad

If you go on holiday abroad, see if you notice any different things people eat and the way they eat them.

A meal to make

Here's a whole meal you can make, which has all the good things you need. Do you know which dish has most protein? Which has lots of vitamin C? Which one is best for your teeth and bones?

Ham salad roll

You need:
- a slice of ham
- some soft cheese
- a stick of celery

Spread the cheese onto the ham.

Lay the celery at one end. Roll the ham around it.

Serve it with some brown bread.

You could put lettuce inside too.

Yoghurt drink

You need:
- a glass of milk
- a pot of fruit yoghurt

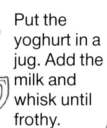

Put the yoghurt in a jug. Add the milk and whisk until frothy.

You could add another fruit.

Banana kebabs

You need:
- a banana • lemon juice • dessicated coconut • a skewer

Peel and cut the banana into rounds.

Soak the rounds in lemon juice.

Dip each round in coconut and thread on the skewer.

Answers: The ham roll has most protein. The banana kebab has most vitamin C. The yoghurt drink is best for your teeth and bones because it has calcium and vitamin D.

24

WHY DO TIGERS HAVE STRIPES?

Mike Unwin

Designed by Sharon Bennett

Illustrated by Robert Morton, Steven Kirk, Gillian Miller, Robert Gillmor, Treve Tamblin and Stuart Trotter

Editor: Helen Edom

Science consultant: Dr Margaret Rostron

CONTENTS

Additional designs by Non Figg

A world of colours

Many animals, such as tigers, have interesting colours or patterns. This book explains how colours and patterns help all kinds of animals' from the biggest elephants to the tiniest insects.

A tiger has a striped pattern. Can you think of any other animals with stripes?

Matching colours

Different animals' colours often match the places where they live. The oryx is an antelope that lives in the desert. Its pale colour matches the sandy background.

In deserts there are few places to hide from enemies. Sandy animals are hard to spot because they blend in. Colours or patterns that help animals to hide are called camouflage.

An oryx is pale and sandy like the desert.

Some desert animals live in holes. When they come out their sandy-coloured camouflage helps them hide from hunters such as hawks and foxes.

Scorpion

Gerbil

Hidden hunters

Most animals run away if they see a hunter coming. Camouflage helps hunters to hide so they can catch other animals to eat.

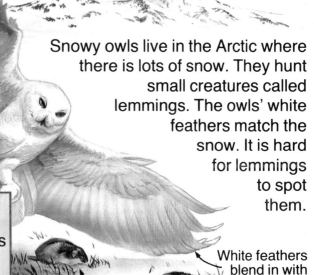

Snowy owls live in the Arctic where there is lots of snow. They hunt small creatures called lemmings. The owls' white feathers match the snow. It is hard for lemmings to spot them.

White feathers blend in with the snow and sky.

Lemmings

Forest greens

Many animals that live in rainforests are green to match the colours of the leaves. This camouflage makes them very hard to see.

Look at the green tree frog in this picture. How many other animals can you spot?

Tree frog

Blue waters

Camouflage is also important under the sea. Many sharks and other fish are coloured blue or grey. This helps them to blend in with the colours underwater.

Blue sharks

27

Patterns

Background colours are not the only kind of camouflage. Patterns also help animals to hide.

Breaking up shapes

A tiger in the zoo looks big, bright and easy to see. But in the forests and long grass where it hunts, a tiger can be hard to spot.

A tiger's stripes seem to break up its shape into small pieces. It is hard to see among the patterns and shadows of the background. This helps it to creep up on deer and other animals.

Seeing in black and white

This black and white picture shows how a leopard looks to an antelope.

Many animals such as antelope cannot see colours. They see in black and white. This makes it very hard for them to make out an animal, such as a leopard, whose pattern breaks up its shape.

Lying in wait

The gaboon viper is a snake that lives on the ground in African forests. Its complicated pattern makes its shape hard to see against the leaves.

Small animals cannot see a gaboon viper lying in wait for them. When they get close, the viper kills them with a bite from its poisonous fangs.

From a distance

The ringed plover lives on beaches. Close up its markings look bright. But from a distance you can only see a pattern that looks like the pebbles.

Ringed plover

If the plover keeps still, it seems to disappear into the stony background. Enemies cannot spot it unless they are close.

Seaweed shapes

The sargassum fish has strange lumps of skin that stick out from its body. These make its shape hard to see. It seems to disappear among the seaweed where it lives.

People hiding

Soldiers wear uniforms with special patterns. This helps them to blend into the background, just like tigers do.

29

Shadows and light

Light and shadow can make animals stand out from their background.

Lying flat

This bird is called a stone curlew. It is well camouflaged, but you can still see its shadow. In daylight, solid things always have shadows. This helps you to see where they are.

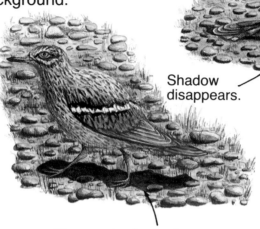

Shadow disappears.

Stone curlew's shadow.

A stone curlew lies flat on the ground so it looks small. This makes its shadow disappear so it is even harder for enemies to spot.

Flat shapes

Some animals have flattened bodies. Enemies do not notice them because they leave hardly any shadow.

Flaps of skin on a gecko's tail make it look flat.

The flying gecko is a lizard that lives on tree trunks. It has a flat body with flaps of skin that press down on the bark. This helps it to hide.

Dark and pale

You can often spot solid things by seeing the light shining on them.

Sunlight makes the top of this rock look lighter than the background.

No sunlight reaches the bottom, so it looks darker than the background.

The impala, like many animals, is coloured dark above and pale below. This is the opposite of the natural light and shadow that fall on its body. It makes the impala harder to pick out from its background.

From below

Many water birds such as puffins are white underneath. They swim on the surface of the water and dive down to catch fish.

From underwater the surface looks bright because of sunlight above it. It is hard for fish to spot puffins from below. Their white undersides are hidden against the bright surface of the water.

Hiding with mirrors

Many sea fish such as shad have shiny silver scales on their sides and bellies. Underwater, these scales work like mirrors. They reflect the colours of the water, so the fish become almost invisible.

31

Disguises

Some animals are shaped to look like other things. This helps them to hide. These insects all have disguises that help them hide in forests.

This caterpillar looks just like a bird dropping, so nothing wants to eat it.

The thorn bug looks just like a thorn on a branch.

The leaf butterfly's folded wings look like a leaf on the forest floor.

The stick insect looks just like twigs.

Standing straight

Animals can help their disguises to work by the way they behave. The tawny frogmouth is a bird with colours like bark. If it is in danger, it points its beak upwards so it looks like a dead branch.

Deadly flowers

The flower mantis is a hunting insect. Its body is the same colour and shape as the flowers where it hides.

Other insects that visit the flower do not notice the mantis lying in wait to catch them.

Like a log

A crocodile in the water can look just like a floating log. This disguise helps it to catch antelope that come to the water to drink.

The crocodile's rough skin looks like old tree bark.

Dressing up

Some animals disguise themselves by decorating their bodies. The sponge crab lives on the sea bed. It holds a sponge on its back with its back legs.

This helps the crab to look like part of the sea bed.

Antelope do not notice the crocodile drifting towards them. When the crocodile gets close enough, it grabs an antelope with its huge jaws and pulls it into the water.

33

Surprises

Some animals stop enemies attacking by tricking or surprising them. They often use colours or patterns to help.

Frightening eyes

Many hunters are frightened if they suddenly see a big pair of eyes.

This swallowtail caterpillar has patterns that look like eyes. Birds think they belong to a bigger, more dangerous creature, so they leave the caterpillar alone.

The caterpillar's real eyes are hidden under here.

A bright flash

The red underwing moth looks well camouflaged on bark. But if it is spotted by a bird, it opens its top wings to show the bright red underneath.

Bark

A sudden flash of red surprises the bird. It leaves the moth alone.

Missing the target

This hairstreak butterfly has a pattern on its wings that looks like another head. Birds peck at the wings by mistake. This gives the butterfly time to escape.

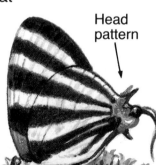

Head pattern

The real head is at this end.

34

Puffing up

Some animals make themselves look bigger to trick enemies. A long-eared owl spreads its wings and puffs up its feathers to frighten enemies away.

This owl looks twice as big as usual.

Playing dead

Some hunters, such as hawks, only attack living creatures. An opossum is a small animal that pretends to be dead when it is in danger. When the danger has gone, the opossum gets up again.

An opossum pretends to be dead by rolling over with its mouth open.

Looking both ways

In India tigers sometimes attack farmers. Tigers are scared by people's faces so they attack from behind. Farmers wear masks on the backs of their heads to scare tigers away.

35

Keep-away colours

Some animals do not try to hide. They have bright colours and patterns that are meant to be seen. These colours are a warning to their enemies.

Remembering colours

Black and yellow patterns are easy for animals to remember. Wasps are bright yellow and black. They can give their enemies a painful sting.

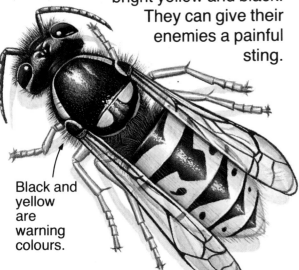

Black and yellow are warning colours.

If a young bird is stung by a wasp, it remembers its pattern. It will not try to catch a wasp again, because it knows that black and yellow things hurt.

Eating bees

A few birds, such as bee-eaters, have found a way to eat bees safely. They are not put off by warning colours. Bee-eaters strike a bee against a branch so its sting is squeezed out and broken.

Being seen

Many poisonous animals do not run away. Instead they show off their warning colours to their enemies.

The deadly poisonous arrow-poison frog does not hop away from enemies like other frogs do. It crawls around slowly so it can easily be seen.

Fierce black and white

The ratel is an African badger. Its white back makes it easy to see. Although it is quite small, it is very fierce and is not afraid of any other animal.

The ratel has strong teeth and claws.

The ratel does not need to keep a look-out for danger like most animals do. Its colours warn enemies that it is too dangerous to attack.

Smelly warning

Skunks are small animals with a bold pattern. They can squirt a nasty, smelly liquid at enemies such as dogs.

A spotted skunk stands up on its front legs to show its pattern. This warns the dog to stay back. If the dog comes closer, the skunk sprays it.

Signals for people

People use warning colours just like animals do. Red often means "hot", "stop" or "danger".

This red tap warns you to be careful because the water is hot.

37

Copying colours

Some animals survive because they have colours and patterns that help them to look like other kinds of animal.

Poisonous or safe?

Can you tell the difference between these two snakes? The coral snake is very poisonous. Its bright colours are a warning.

The king snake looks like a coral snake, but it is not poisonous at all. If you look hard you can see that its pattern is slightly different.

Other animals are afraid to attack the king snake because it looks like a poisonous coral snake.

Coral snake

King snake

Which is the wasp?

Some insects look just like wasps, even though they do not really have stings. Most animals do not attack these insects because their colours remind them of stinging wasps.

Can you guess which insect is a wasp? Look on page 98 for the answer.

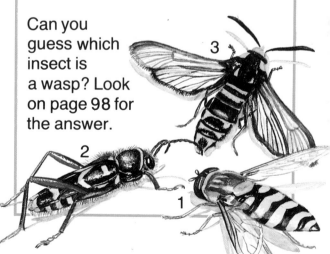

3

2

1

Ant antics

Most animals leave ants alone because they bite and sting. Some kinds of spider look and behave like ants to fool their enemies.

Ants

The spider holds up two of its eight legs so it appears to have only six legs, like an ant.

The spider's upright front legs look like an ant's feelers.

Getting close

The cleaner fish helps bigger fish by cleaning unwanted dirt and lice from their skin.

Cleaner fish

The sabre-toothed blenny looks like a cleaner fish, but it is really a hunter that tricks other fish.

Sabre-toothed blenny

Big fish let the blenny come near because they think it is a cleaner fish. But the blenny attacks them and takes bites out of their fins.

Whose egg?

Can you tell which of these eggs does not belong?

Reed warbler

The middle one is a cuckoo's egg. The rest belong to the reed warbler.

The cuckoo lays its egg in a reed warbler's nest. It is the same colour as the eggs that are already there. The warblers think the cuckoo's egg is their own so they look after it.

39

Signals

Some kinds of animals use colours and patterns as signals to each other.

Danger

A rabbit has a short, fluffy, white tail. If it sees an enemy such as a fox, it runs quickly back to its burrow, flashing its tail in the air.

The white tail is a signal to other rabbits. It says "danger!"

Follow my leader

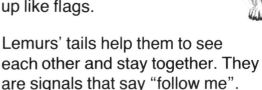

Ring-tailed lemurs are animals with long black and white tails. When a group of lemurs is on the move, they hold their tails up like flags.

Lemurs' tails help them to see each other and stay together. They are signals that say "follow me".

Getting angry

A tiger has bold, white spots on its ears. If one tiger is angry with another, it turns the backs of its ears forwards to show the white spots.

The white spots are a signal that warns other tigers to keep away.

Looking different

Colours can make it easier to tell similar animals apart. This helps animals to recognize others of their own kind.

Goldfinch

Chaffinch

These are the wings of two different finches. Their shape and size are the same, but the patterns and colours help to tell them apart.

Being fed

Baby birds in nests wait for their parents to bring food. The babies' mouths are brightly coloured inside.

These baby great tits have bright orange mouths.

When a parent arrives with food, the babies open their mouths wide to show the colour inside. This is a signal to the parent. It says "feed me!"

People's colours

People also use colours to tell each other apart. All sports teams wear their own colours. This stops them getting mixed up with each other.

Different soccer teams wear different colours.

Mysterious lights

Hatchet fish live deep at the bottom of the sea, where it is very dark. They have small patches on their bodies that light up and flash on and off.

Scientists think these lights could be signals to help hatchet fish recognize each other.

41

Showing off

Many male animals have bright colours to make them look attractive to females. This helps to bring the male and female together to breed.

Bright or brown

Male and female birds often look different from each other.

A male golden pheasant has beautifully coloured feathers which he shows off to attract a female.

The female pheasant has much duller colours. This helps her to hide when she is protecting her eggs and chicks.

Risky colours

Bright colours can also attract enemies. In spring a male paradise whydah's bright colours are easy to spot, and his long tail makes it hard for him to fly away.

After the whydah has found a female he loses his colours and long tail. For the rest of the year he stays plain brown.

Putting on a show

Some male birds put on a show to attract females. Every spring, male ruffs gather together. They puff up their feathers and fight. Females choose the males that put on the best show.

Three different male ruffs fighting.

Colourful lizards

A male anolis lizard has an orange flap of skin under his throat. Usually it is folded up. But sometimes the lizard puffs it out and nods his head to show off the colour.

The bright throat attracts females. It also warns other males to keep out of the area.

Fierce faces

Mandrills are African monkeys. A male mandrill has a colourful face that gets brighter when he is looking for a female. The biggest and fiercest males are brightest of all.

A female mandrill chooses the male with the brightest colours. Other males keep away from him.

Collecting colours

A male bowerbird attracts a female by building a pile of twigs called a bower. He then decorates it with shells, flowers and bright, shiny things.

A female bowerbird chooses the male with the best bower. She then builds a nest and lays the eggs.

43

Making colours

Fur, feathers, scales and skin can be all sorts of different colours. Animals get these colours in many different ways.

Colours from food

Flamingos' feathers are pink because of a colouring called carotene which is found in water plants. Flamingos get carotene by eating tiny water animals that feed on these plants.

Often flamingos in zoos are not as pink as wild ones, because there is not enough carotene in their food.

Shiny colours

Many birds, such as sunbirds, have bright, shiny feathers. These change colour when light falls on them from different directions.

This sunbird's feathers change from blue to green as the light shines on them.

Killed for colours

Some snakes are becoming rare because people kill them for their beautiful skins.

This bag is made from the skin of a python.

Growing green

Animals do not normally grow green fur. But this sloth looks green. This is because tiny green plants called algae grow in its fur.

Jigsaw

Butterflies' patterns are made by thousands of tiny different-coloured scales that fit together.

Peacock butterfly scales

This is how the wing of a peacock butterfly looks close up. Can you see how the scales are arranged in rows?

Black fur

Animals have a kind of colouring in their bodies called melanin. Melanin makes dark colours in fur and skin.

A black panther is really a leopard born with more melanin than usual. Its fur is black. But if you look closely you can still see its spots.

White all over

Sometimes animals are born white. They have no melanin so they cannot make dark colours. These are called albino animals.

An albino blackbird has white feathers.

45

Changes

Some animals can change their colours. Chameleons are lizards that change the colour of their skin to match different backgrounds.

This chameleon has a green pattern when it is hiding among leaves.

On sandy ground the same chameleon turns brown. It is always very hard to spot.

Sole survivor

The sole is a flatfish. It hides from enemies by lying flat on the sea bed. Its colour depends on where it lies.

This sole is the colour and pattern of the pebbles on which it is lying. If it moves onto mud, it becomes a muddy colour.

Sudden changes

If an octopus is in danger, different colours flash over its body. This surprises enemies and gives the octopus time to escape.

Colours also show how an octopus feels. For example, an angry octopus often turns red.

White for winter

Many animals that live in cold parts of the world turn white in winter. At the end of summer an Arctic fox sheds its brown fur and grows a white coat.

Fox in summer   Fox in winter

White fur helps the fox to hide during winter when the ground is covered in snow. In spring the fox's brown fur grows back again.

After the fire

In Africa, fires often change the colour of grassland by burning it black. Some kinds of grasshopper can turn from green to black to match the colour of the ground.

Before the fire the grasshoppers were green like this one.

Colours of the land

The colour of an African elephant's skin can change, depending on the soil where it lives. This is because it covers itself in dirt and mud to cool down.

This elephant lives in a place with red soil, so it has reddish skin.

Animal puzzle

Here are eight different parts and patterns from animals that you can find in this part of the book.

Can you work out which animals they come from? The answers are at the bottom of the page.

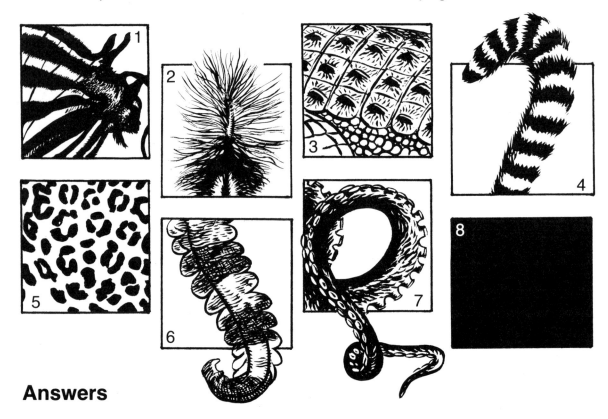

Answers

1. Hairstreak butterfly 2. Spotted skunk 3. Crocodile 4. Ring-tailed lemur 5. Leopard 6. Flying gecko 7. Octopus 8. Black panther on a dark night.

48

WHY ARE PEOPLE DIFFERENT?

Susan Meredith

Designed by Lindy Dark

Illustrated by Annabel Spenceley and Kuo Kang Chen

Consultants: Dr Michael Hitchcock,
Indu Patel and Dr John Kesby

CONTENTS

What is a person?

Have you ever wondered why you are what you are? Why are you the same as other people in so many ways, yet different too?

There are millions of different kinds of living things in the world.

People everywhere are like they are for two main reasons. One is that they take after their parents. The other is that they are affected by the sort of life they live.

What made you a person, not some other living thing like a cat or a daisy, are thousands of tiny things inside you called genes. People's genes are different from animal or plant genes.

Where you live

Your genes are only part of the story. You are the way you are also because of where you live: your surroundings. Another word for surroundings is environment. Your environment affects the way you live. This picture shows life in a part of West Africa.

These women are pounding vegetables called yams. They are made into a kind of porridge.

Young children stay close to their mothers.

This woman is carrying pots.

You got, or inherited, your genes from your parents.

Your parents inherited their genes from their parents.

Genes are the instructions which make your body work in the way it does. Everyone gets their genes from their parents, at the moment when they start to grow inside their mother.

Some things about you, like the way you look, depend a lot on your genes.

People all look different because of their genes.

Although everybody has genes, they are arranged in a different pattern in different people. That is one of the reasons why one person is not quite like another.

One big family

Everyone everywhere is really part of the same huge family which scientists call humans or human beings.

Everyone's bodies and brains are all made in the same way.

Overhanging thatch keeps rain off the walls.

Houses are made of mud bricks which have been dried in the sun. They are nice and cool inside.

The weather is hot. Long, loose cotton clothes help people keep cool.

Oven

Where did people come from?

Jellyfish have been around for hundreds of millions of years; people for only about two million.

Creatures which were a bit like small apes lived about 10 million years ago.

There have not always been people in the world. There were plants and animals long before any humans. So where did people come from?

Most scientists think that living things gradually change, or evolve, over a very long time. They think people evolved from ape-like creatures.*

Out of Africa

Experts think that the first people evolved in Africa. They think they gradually spread all over the world from there, in the directions of the arrows on this map.

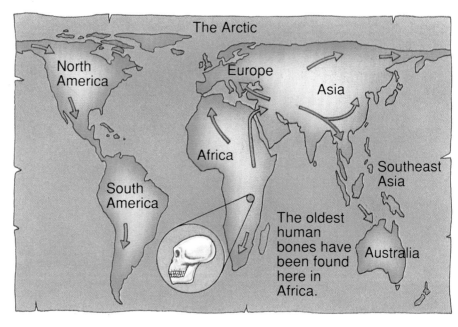

The Arctic

North America

Europe

Asia

Africa

South America

Southeast Asia

The oldest human bones have been found here in Africa.

Australia

52 *Some people do not believe things evolve. They believe God created people as they are today.

The first people

Stick

Stone

Humans had evolved by two million years ago. They walked on two legs and had hands which could use tools. They hunted animals and gathered wild plant foods.

Chimps

Young humans are very much like young chimps.

The animals people are most like today are chimps. Nine out of every ten human genes are almost the same as chimp genes. The main difference is that people are brainier.

Your oldest relations

The first people whose bodies and brains were like yours evolved about a hundred thousand years ago. They made many weapons and tools, and could probably talk. This picture shows life in a cool place.

These people hunted with spears.

They lived in caves and in shelters made from animal skins.

They made fires: for warmth, for cooking and to frighten off wild animals.

They sewed animal skins to wear.

53

Taking after your parents

The genes you get from your parents control the way your body lives, works and grows. The picture below shows just a few of the things about you that depend on your genes.

The way you live cannot change your genes. It can affect how your body copes with some genes though.

Your hair: whether it is dark or fair, curly or straight.

Your eye colour

Your face

Your voice

Your skin colour

Some people seem to inherit genes which make them more at risk of tooth decay than others.

If they do not eat much sweet food and clean their teeth very thoroughly, their teeth may stay healthy.

How genes work

Most things about you are decided by several genes. A few, such as hair and eye colour, depend mainly on one gene from each parent. The example on the right will give you an idea of how genes work.

Your hair colour depends on the mixture of your two hair colour genes. A dark hair gene is dominant (strong). It blocks out genes for other colours. A fair hair gene blocks out a red hair gene.

Jessica's mother has a dark and a red hair gene. Her dark gene blocks out her red.

Jessica's father has a fair and a red hair gene. His fair gene blocks out his red.

Jessica happened to inherit both her mother's and father's red hair genes.

Where are your genes?

Your body is made of millions of tiny living parts called cells. Your genes are stored in your cells, on special threads called chromosomes.

Chromosome ——

Cell

Your cells have 46 chromosomes each: 23 from your mother, 23 from your father.

Chromosomes are made of a chemical (DNA) which looks like a twisted ladder. There are hundreds of genes on each chromosome.

About 250 rungs on the ladder make one gene.

The rungs are arranged in a different order in different people. This is what makes everybody unique.

Exactly which of your parents' genes you get seems to be a matter of chance. That is why brothers and sisters do not always seem alike.

Only identical twins have exactly the same genes.

Genes or environment?

Simon walks with his feet turned out. Is this because of his genes or because he has copied his Dad? Nobody knows.

There is a lot that is still not known about genes. Nobody really knows whether some things about you depend mainly on your genes, your environment or both.

People and the weather

Living things evolve (change) to fit in with their environment. This is called adapting to the environment. Things that do not adapt, die.

Things that do adapt, survive and pass on their genes to their children. Gradually there come to be more and more of the well adapted things.

Woolly mammoths were well suited to life in the ice age. When the weather warmed up, they did not adapt and died out.

Humans evolved skilful hands and good brains. This makes them well adapted to their environment.

Body build

Over a very long time, people's genes have helped them adapt to the weather in different parts of the world. Groups of people have come to look different from one another because of this.

Plump people were better adapted to the cold. They survived and passed on their plumpness genes to their children.

The children passed on the genes to their children. Today nearly all Arctic people are plump.

Slim people were not adapted to living in the frozen Arctic. They did not have enough body fat, which helps keep you warm.

Extra fat on the eyelids protects the eyes from the cold and glare of the snow.

Dark or fair skin?

In very sunny places people evolved dark skin. This blocks out some of the sun's harmful rays.

Dark skin helps protect people from too much sun.

In cloudier places people did not need so much protection from the sun. They evolved fairer skin.

People need some sunshine because it gives them vitamin D.

Ways of life

It is not only people's genes which have adapted to the weather. People have also adapted their way of life. Clothes, houses, even food and jobs can all depend on the weather.

Head-dress and veil give protection from the sun and wind of the Sahara Desert.

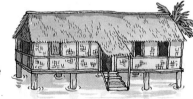

Houses are built on stilts in Southeast Asia, where there are often floods.

Living apart

Groups of people came to look different not only because of the weather but also because they lived far apart.

Most people used not to travel far, so they did not meet people from other parts of the world.

Today people from opposite sides of the world marry each other. Their genes get mixed together in their children.

57

Learning to fit in

Right from the time you are a baby, you have to start learning to fit in with the people around you. Different people have to learn to fit into very different kinds of world, depending on where they are growing up.

Showing the soles of your feet when you are sitting down is very impolite in Arab countries.

Eating in public places is impolite in Japan.

How you are expected to behave depends on your own family's way of thinking and on the general ways and rules of the place where you live.

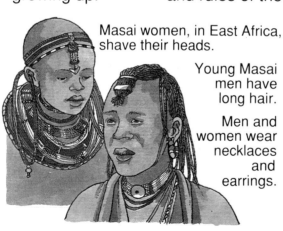

Masai women, in East Africa, shave their heads.

Young Masai men have long hair.

Men and women wear necklaces and earrings.

How you dress depends on what people in the place where you live think is suitable and attractive.

Someone who likes being outdoors may not much enjoy city life.

How happily people fit in depends on the kind of person they are and the type of environment they live in.

58

How do people learn?

Children learn how to behave by following the example of people they admire such as parents, teachers and friends.

Behaving well is sometimes rewarded by smiles, praise or even presents. This encourages someone to be good another time.

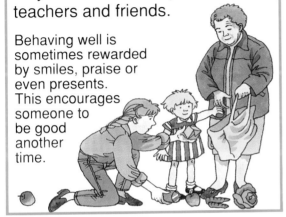

Babies

Young babies do not fit in all that well with other people. When they need something, they just cry for it. This is the only way they have of telling people something is wrong.

Babies cannot wait for things, or imagine how other people feel.

Children

As babies grow up, they learn to fit in, for example, eating at mealtimes, not just when they are hungry.

At school, you learn skills which will help you to cope with life in the wider world outside your family.

You also learn by playing with other children, for example, how to share and take turns in games.

Making a living

Everybody everywhere needs things like food and shelter. Most people have to earn money to meet their needs. The work people do depends largely on where they live and what kind of jobs there are in the area.

Farming

Most people in the world live in villages rather than towns and make their living by farming.

In some parts of the world machines are used.

Harvesting rice in the USA.

Harvesting rice in Southeast Asia.

In places where most people are farmers (Africa, Asia, South America) a lot of the work is still done by hand.

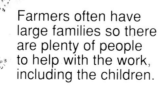

Farmers often have large families so there are plenty of people to help with the work, including the children.

In places like Europe, North America, Japan and Australia there is a lot of industry. Many people work in factories, making things to be sold, or in offices. They get paid a wage.

People in industrial places often live in small families. They may move to find work.

In some places farmers do not get paid but keep some of what they grow.

60

Herding animals

In a few places, where it is too dry to do much else, some people herd animals for their living. They have to keep moving from place to place to find water and grazing land for the animals. These people are called nomads. They get most of what they need from their animals.

These people in Central Asia live in felt tents. (Felt is made from animals' wool.)

The tents are warm, and can be taken down and moved fairly easily.

The people keep sheep, goats, yaks, horses and camels. They sell animals to buy things they need such as wheat.

From the animals they get meat, milk and cheese; and wool and skins to make into clothes, tents and blankets.

They use the animals for getting around.

Fishing

Some people by the sea depend on fishing for their living, especially in places where there is no farming or industry nearby.

In the Arctic it is too cold for crops to grow. This man is fishing through a hole in the ice.

Other jobs

Some jobs are done all over the world, for example, teaching, nursing, or office work. Others are only done in certain places.

Tea will only grow on hills in warm wet places. It is grown in India and China.

Picking tea

61

Talking to each other

There are thousands of different languages spoken in the world today. The language with most speakers is Chinese. In second place is English.

How did language begin?

Mammoth

People gradually began to give meanings to the sounds they made.

Nobody is sure when or how people started to talk. They may have begun with noises such as grunts, and signs such as pointing.

Body language

In Indonesia it is rude to point with your finger. People use their thumb.

You do not only talk in words. You also use your face and body. Some things, like laughing and crying, mean the same everywhere. Some do not.

Borrowing words

As people move around the world, their language goes with them. Words from one language often creep into another. Below are just a few words which have come into English from other languages:

potato (Native American), *anorak* (Inuit), *tea* (Chinese), *jungle* (Hindi), *garage* (French), *pyjamas* (Urdu), *orange* (Arabic), *robot* (Czech), *coach* (Hungarian).

Language families

Guten Morgen

Good morning

Goede morgen

German   English   Dutch

Many languages are related. French, Spanish and Italian all evolved from Latin, the language of the Ancient Romans. English is similar to German and Dutch.

62

Learning to talk

By the time they are one, most babies can speak a few words and understand many more.

Babies' babblings include all the sounds it is possible for the human voice to make.

Young children gradually learn to speak the same language as their parents just by hearing and copying the sounds they make.

Same but different

The same language is often spoken differently in different places.

Even the same person can speak differently in different situations. Do you talk the same way to your friends as you do to your teachers?

Writing

There are over 50 different alphabets. Most West European languages have used the Roman alphabet since the time the Romans ruled the area. On the right are some letters from different alphabets.

Chinese does not have an alphabet like that of most other languages.

This one symbol means horse in Chinese.

63

Moving around

Right from the time the first people moved out of Africa, groups of people have left one area and gone to settle in another. Journeys made long ago help to explain why people live where they do now.

Hunger

Sometimes people move because their crops die through drought (lack of rain), floods or disease.

In Ireland the potato crop failed in 1845 and people were starving. Thousands left for America or England.

Where from?

As people move around, they take their ideas and the things they use with them. Here are a few examples of where things started out.

Guinea pigs Potatoes }	South America
Fireworks Ice cream }	China
Arithmetic Oranges }	The Middle East

Slavery

In the 1600s and 1700s, millions of Africans were forced to go to America and work as slaves in the fields where sugar, tobacco and cotton were grown.

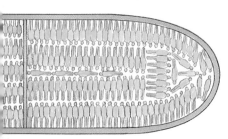

The slaves were packed like sardines on ships for the journey. Many died.

Plan of a slave ship.

Jobs

People often move from the countryside into towns to find work. Sometimes they move to a completely foreign country, often one which has close links with their own.

In the 1950s, many doctors moved from India to Britain, where more doctors were needed.

Power

There have been many times when one group of people has moved in on another and tried to rule them.

In the 1500s, Spain conquered many parts of South and Central America and ruled them for years.

Spanish is still spoken in those countries (shown yellow on this map), making it the third most spoken language in the world.

Brazil (Portuguese spoken here.)

Land

Sometimes people have moved to find new land to live on and farm. This has often led to trouble.

In the 1800s, many Europeans went to North America. There were fierce battles as they tried to take land there.

European settlers

Native Americans

The Native Americans were pushed into living only in certain areas called reservations.

Disagreements

Sometimes people are badly treated just because of what they believe or even who they are. This often happens in wartime.

Many Jews fled from Central and Eastern Europe at the time of World War II to escape being killed.

Prisoners

In 1788, the British government began sending prisoners far from home to Australia as a punishment.

Many stayed and made their living in Australia when their time in prison was over.

65

What people believe

People's beliefs depend a lot on what their families believe and on the religion and ideas that are taught in the place where they grow up. There are many different religions. Some have a lot in common.

Festivals

The Japanese Shinto religion teaches that gods are in nature.

People pray at places like this.

Many religions involve believing in some kind of god or gods. Believers may pray to their god, often asking for help or giving praise and thanks.

Religions try to explain how the world and people were made. It is only fairly recently that scientists have figured out the idea that living things evolved.*

The Christian and Jewish religions teach that God made the world and the first man and woman: Adam and Eve.

This Muslim is going from door to door, collecting rice for the poor.

Religions give rules for how to behave. For example, Muslims are expected to give to the poor and old.

*See page 52.

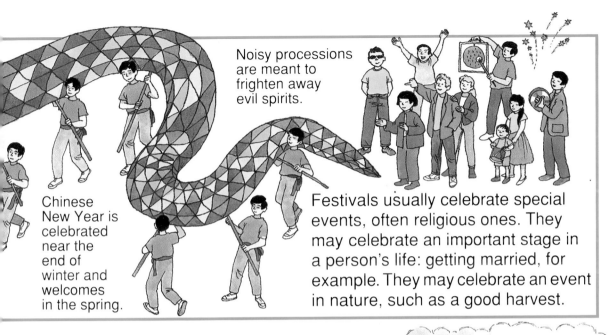

Noisy processions are meant to frighten away evil spirits.

Chinese New Year is celebrated near the end of winter and welcomes in the spring.

Festivals usually celebrate special events, often religious ones. They may celebrate an important stage in a person's life: getting married, for example. They may celebrate an event in nature, such as a good harvest.

Many religions involve believing in some kind of life after death. Hinduism, for example, teaches that people are reborn into the world. If you are good in this life, your next life will be a better one.

Hindu holy men give up their possessions and try to live a good and simple life.

Politics

People with different political ideas disagree about the best way to organize and rule a country.

Greens believe it is all-important to improve the environment before it is ruined totally.

In some places people have no say in who rules them. In most countries elections are held. Then people can vote for those they think will run the country best.

Voting in India

67

People in groups

People everywhere are much more alike than they are different. However, it is sometimes interesting to think about people as different groups.

Male and female

Without the bodily differences between men and women, human beings would soon die out because no babies would be made.

What makes the difference between a boy and a girl is just one chromosome out of the 46 you have in each cell in your body.

Ethnic groups

People of the same ethnic group have relations who lived in the same part of the world long ago. They often share the same language, customs and beliefs.

People whose relations originally came from Britain often eat British Christmas dinner in Australia.

The way men and women behave differently and do different tasks has a lot to do with where they live and how they were brought up.

In Bali, Southeast Asia, women do the heavy work on building sites.

Many crane drivers in Dutch ports are women.

Friends

Friends may be quite different in some ways.

People may become friends because they have similar hobbies, interests or ideas; or just because they like each other. Friends often help each other.

Young people

Young people* are learning to manage without their parents. They often go around in groups; this gives them a feeling of belonging while being free of their families.

Old people

Old people may not be as fit as they once were but the things they have learned during their long life can be very interesting and useful to younger people.

Countries

People living in the same country live under the same government and have to obey its laws. Laws vary from one country to another.

ALCOHOL FORBIDDEN IN THIS COUNTRY

Alcoholic drink is banned in some countries.

Disabled people

Disabled people cannot easily do some of the things most people take for granted. There are different types of disability. Some can be overcome.

A wheelchair marathon

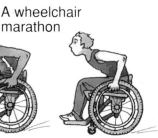

*To find out about children, see page 59.

One world

Humans have always had to adapt to survive and still need to adapt today. The main challenge now is for people to change their way of life before they damage the environment so much that they can no longer live in it. Here are some of the things humans can do to improve their environment.

Sewage works

Find new kinds of energy which do not pollute the air people breathe. (Machines need energy to work.)

Wind turbines like this can be used to make electricity, without pollution.

Make things from materials which do not harm the environment when thrown away. Better still, make them from materials which can be re-used.

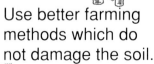

Bottle bank

Use better farming methods which do not damage the soil.

Clean sewage (waste from toilets and drains) properly so it does not pollute rivers and seas. Half the people in the world do not have clean, safe drinking water.

Stop dumping harmful chemical waste from factories, farms and even homes in rivers and seas.

Rare orchid

Stop letting wild animals and plants die out. Besides being important in themselves, some may be useful to humans as new types of food or medicine.

Stop cutting down forests. This destroys the homes of animals and plants, damages the soil and even causes changes in the weather.

Rich and poor

About a quarter of the people in the world own more than three-quarters of the world's wealth. Most people in the parts of the world shown green on this map are quite well off. Most people in the parts shown yellow are poor. Many people think that

things should be shared out more fairly.

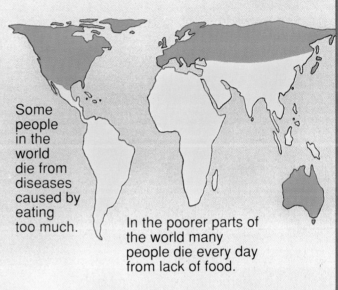

Some people in the world die from diseases caused by eating too much.

In the poorer parts of the world many people die every day from lack of food.

The future

Adapting will not be easy. It will take hard work and goodwill. People in rich countries do not always want to alter their comfortable way of life.

Leaving the car at home saves energy and reduces pollution.

A shower wastes less water than a bath.

SAVE THE EARTH

Humans know what some of the problems are that face them. With the best brains of any living creature, they may well be able to find solutions.

Useful words

Ancestors

Relations who lived before you, from your grandparents back; relations from whom you are descended (see *Descendants* opposite).

Culture

The beliefs, customs (see below) and general way of life of a group of people.

Music is part of people's culture.

Indian sitar

Custom

A habit, usual way of doing something, tradition.

It is a custom in many countries to take a present to a birthday party.

Descendants

The children, grandchildren, great grandchildren, and so on, of someone. You are a descendant of your parents, grandparents and so on back.

Queen Elizabeth II is a descendant of Queen Victoria.

Environment

Everything that surrounds a living thing and affects its life. Your environment includes the area where you live, your home, school, family, friends and possessions.

Inherit

1 To have passed on to you in your genes by your parents and ancestors.

He inherited his grandad's curly hair.

2 To be left something by someone when they die, for example, money or gold rings.

WHAT MAKES YOU ILL?

Mike Unwin & Kate Woodward

Designed by Non Figg
Illustrated by Annabel Spenceley and Kuo Kang Chen

Editor: Susan Meredith

Consultant: Dr Kevan Thorley

CONTENTS

Additional designs by Lindy Dark

All about being ill

Most of the time you probably feel well. Your body can do lots of things without you even thinking about them.

Your brain lets you think clearly.

Most of the time you are happy and feel comfortable inside.

Your skin looks smooth and healthy.

You feel energetic and want to run around and play.

Your arms and legs feel strong.

You get hungry if you have not eaten for a while.

Ill or well?

You can usually tell if you are ill because things feel wrong with your body. These things are called symptoms. You can often tell what is wrong by the kind of symptoms you have.

You may feel hot one minute, then cold the next.

Your tummy may feel shaky and you may need to be sick.

You might feel tired and achy and want to lie down.

You feel miserable, and do not want to join in your friends' games.

You might have a pain somewhere.

You may lose your appetite.

74

What is pain?

Having a pain is one way your body tells you something is wrong.

Sometimes you can easily see what is wrong because of where it hurts.

Sometimes you have a pain in one place when really the problem is somewhere else. Tonsillitis causes a tummy ache, even though your tonsils are in your throat.

Getting better

Your body is good at getting better by itself. You can help it mend by resting. There are lots of ways to keep busy while you rest.

Watching TV

Playing games

Reading

Listening to music

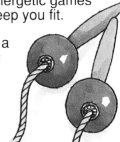

Plenty of love and attention from your family or friends can make you feel better too.

If resting doesn't help, and you don't get better on your own, you may have to visit your doctor.

Keeping well

Looking after yourself helps you stay well. Eating the right food and exercising keep you fit. Being fit helps you fight illness and get better more quickly if you are ill.

Sports and energetic games keep you fit.

Fruit is a healthy food to eat.

Why do you get ill?

People become ill for many different reasons. Most everyday illnesses are caused by germs. Your body usually fights germs off but sometimes they make you ill. This is called having an infection.

There are many different kinds of germ. They cause different symptoms of infection.

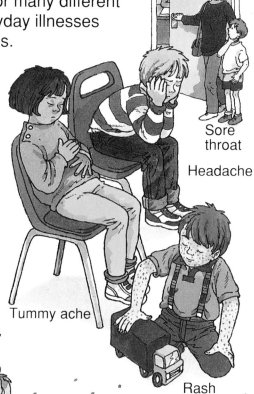

Sore throat

Headache

Tummy ache

Rash

Sneezing sprays millions of germs into the air.

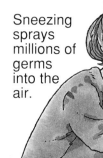

Most germs are spread through the air. When you have a cold you breathe out germs all the time. If people around you breathe them in they may catch your cold.

Where you live

Where you live can affect your health. For example, traffic fumes and factory smoke can pollute the air you breathe. This can make people ill.

Accidents

Sometimes accidents can hurt you or make you ill. Many accidents happen at home.

Falling can give you cuts or bruises or even break your bones.

Hot things can burn you. Always be careful with hot food.

Feelings

Your feelings can make you ill too. Worrying may upset your tummy and make you feel sick.

Feeling nervous about your first day at a new school can make you feel ill.

Family illnesses

Some illnesses tend to run in families. Scientists now know someone is more likely to get asthma if one of their parents has it. Asthma makes it difficult to breathe properly.

People with asthma can take medicine to help them run around and play sports.

Allergies

Ordinary things like cat hair, pollen from plants, and certain foods make some people feel poorly. This is called having an allergy.

An allergy to strawberries can give you a rash.

77

What is a germ?

Germs are tiny, living things. They are everywhere: in the air you breathe, on your skin, in your food and on the things you touch.

There are germs inside your body all the time. Most of them don't do you any harm. Some can even be helpful, but others make you ill.

The three main kinds of germs are called bacteria, viruses and fungi.

Germs are so tiny you need a microscope to see them.

Some useful bacteria live in your tummy. They help you to digest your food.

Bacteria

Bacteria are so tiny that over a thousand could fit on a pinhead. Some can cause illnesses such as ear and skin infections.

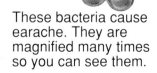

These bacteria cause earache. They are magnified many times so you can see them.

Viruses

Viruses are over a million times smaller than bacteria. They cause many common infections such as colds, tummy upsets and sore throats.

If you look at viruses through very strong microscopes, you can see their strange shapes.

This kind of virus causes sore throats.

Keeping germs out

Your body is built to keep harmful germs out as much as possible. This picture shows how your body protects you.

Eyelashes stop dirt and germs from getting into your eyes.

You have tears in your eyes all the time. They help wash out germs.

Tiny hairs in your nose catch germs you breathe in.

Your skin keeps germs out as long as you have no cuts or scratches.

Germs come out of your nose in slimy stuff called mucus, when you sneeze or blow your nose.

Your mouth and throat are always wet and slippery so that germs don't get stuck there.

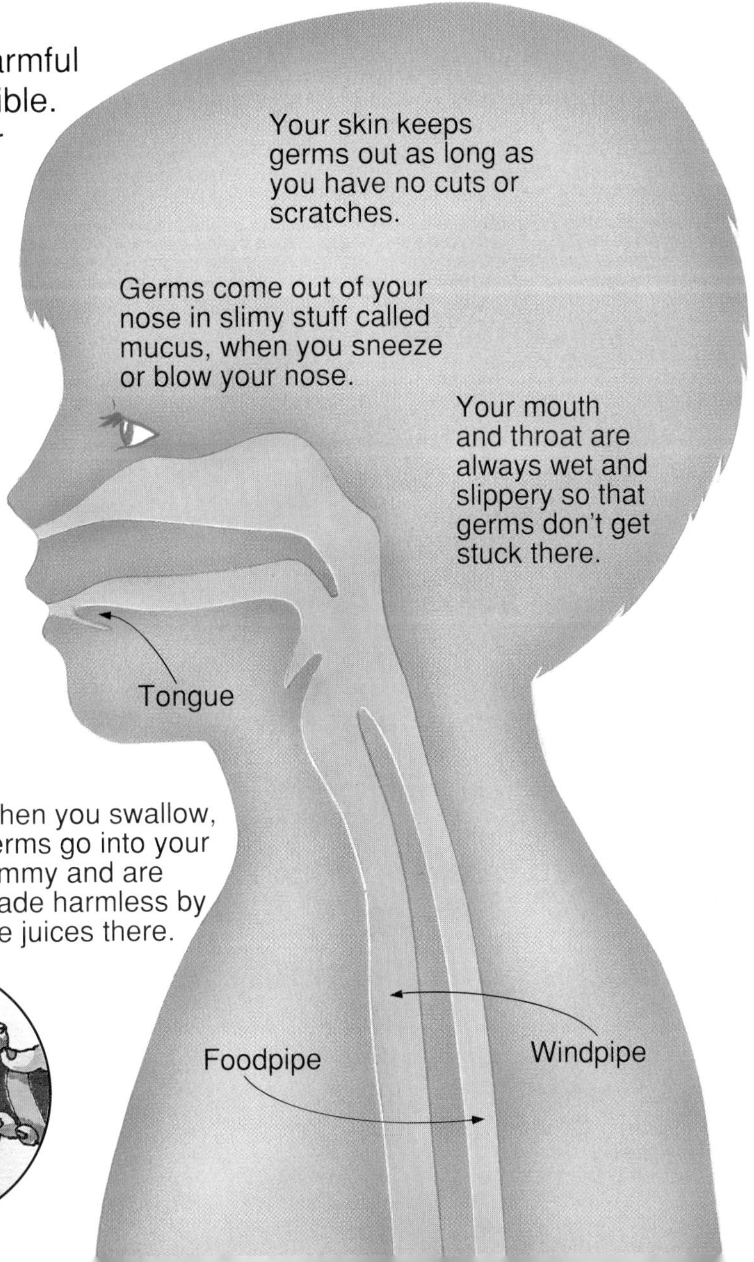

Tongue

Fungi

These are germs which grow on your body and cause infections. Athlete's foot is a fungus which can grow between your toes. It makes your skin look sore and flaky.

You can get rid of athlete's foot with special powder.

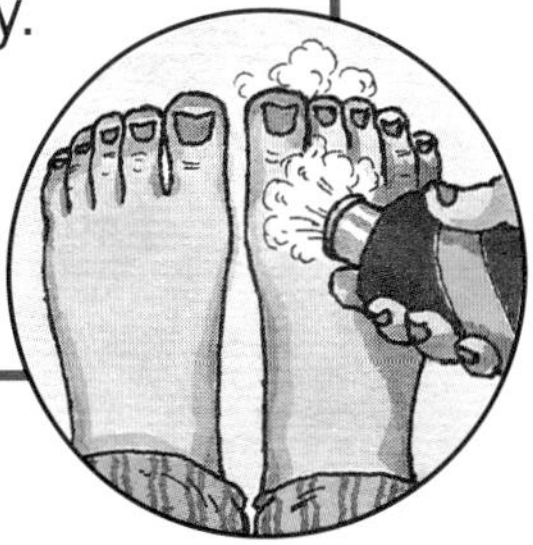

When you swallow, germs go into your tummy and are made harmless by the juices there.

Foodpipe

Windpipe

Germ attack

Your whole body is made up of millions of tiny living parts called cells. When germs such as bacteria or viruses get into your body they start to multiply and feed off your cells. This makes you feel ill.

Bacteria invasion

Your body is a warm, damp place with plenty of food, so bacteria grow and spread quickly inside you. Within hours there can be millions in one small part of your body.

Some bacteria attack your cells by giving off poisons. These can also spread infection around your body in your blood.

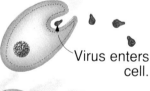

This is what cells from your skin look like through a very strong microscope.

Cell

Poisons

Bacteria

Bacteria attack cell with poisons.

Virus invasion

Viruses attack by getting inside a cell. The cell becomes a kind of factory for making new viruses.

Virus enters cell.

New viruses are made inside cell.

Cells die and viruses set out to invade new cells.

Germs and symptoms

Symptoms are caused both by germs damaging your cells, and by the way your body fights back. Different germs cause symptoms in different parts of your body.

An area infected by bacteria, such as an aching tooth, often feels sore and swollen.

Your temperature rises as your body starts to fight the germs. This is an early sign of infection.

Colds and flu often start with a sore throat because the viruses that cause them start in your throat.

Cleaning cuts and protecting them with a plaster or bandage helps to stop bacteria from getting in.

A medicine called paracetamol helps lower your temperature.

In the blood

Your blood is always flowing inside you. It takes food and oxygen around your body. But it can also help spread any infections that get into your blood.

Getting better

Medicines called antibiotics can help treat illnesses caused by bacteria. No medicines can get rid of viruses. Your body fights them in its own way.

Fighting back

When you get an infection your body fights off the invading germs. In your blood there are special cells to try and stop them from spreading further.

In your blood

This page shows a close-up picture of blood vessels. These are the tubes that carry blood around your body. Blood contains millions of cells in a liquid called plasma. Red blood cells carry food and oxygen. White blood cells have the job of killing germs.

Plasma

White blood cell

Red blood cell

The germ eaters

When germs damage your cells, more blood flows to the infected place. White blood cells then devour the germs.

Germ

1. White blood cell sticks to germs.

2. White blood cell surrounds germs.

3. Germs are digested inside.

Flushing out germs

Lymph is a liquid that runs around your body in a network of tubes. It carries dead germs and cells to swellings called lymph nodes. Here, white blood cells clean them out of the lymph.

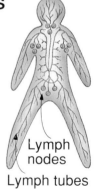

Lymph nodes

Lymph tubes

Lymph nodes, especially in your neck, can feel sore and swollen while you are fighting germs.

Permanent protection

During an infection, special white blood cells called lymphocytes kill germs using chemicals known as antibodies.

Antibody

1. Antibodies hold onto germ.

2. Germ bursts open and dies.

Germ

Antibodies can recognize germs that have attacked you before. They stay in your body to stop the same germs from attacking again. This means you only catch most infections once. Being protected like this is called being immune.

Immunization

Immunization is a way of making you immune to an infectious illness without your ever having to catch it.

When you are immunized, you are given a tiny dose of a germ. The dose is too weak to make you ill, but it helps your body produce the antibodies that will protect you against that illness in the future.

Babies are usually given injections that immunize them against some serious illnesses.

83

Allergies

An allergy is when your body fights ordinary things as if they were germs. This can cause symptoms such as a rash, wheezing or tummy ache. Anything that causes an allergy in somebody is called an allergen.

What happens

When an allergen invades the body of an allergic person, white blood cells send out antibodies to fight it. A chemical called histamine is produced, which causes the allergic symptoms.

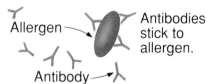

Allergen

Antibodies stick to allergen.

Antibody

Histamine

White blood cell

White blood cell produces histamine.

84

Breathing

Some people are allergic to things they breathe in, such as dust, pollen, feathers or pet hairs.

Hay fever can be caused by an allergy to pollen. It makes you sneeze and your eyes become watery and itchy.

What is asthma?

Asthma can be caused by an allergy. It makes it difficult to breathe air into your lungs, so you wheeze or cough. Here you can see what happens.

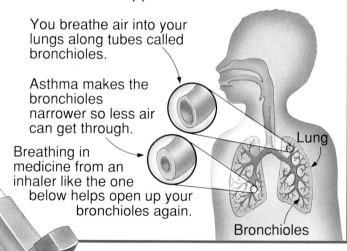

You breathe air into your lungs along tubes called bronchioles.

Asthma makes the bronchioles narrower so less air can get through.

Breathing in medicine from an inhaler like the one below helps open up your bronchioles again.

Lung

Bronchioles

Touching

Some people have to be careful what they wear against their skin. Metal, for instance in earrings, and material such as wool, can cause a rash.

An itchy rash called eczema is sometimes caused by washing powder or soap.

Metal

Wool

Eating

Some people are allergic to certain foods. Eating them can cause allergic symptoms including a tummy ache or rash. Food allergy can play a part in asthma.

These foods can cause allergies in some people.

Milk

Seafood

Chocolate

Treating allergies

You cannot catch allergies from other people. The best protection against them is for people to try to avoid things they know they are allergic to.

It is hard to avoid allergens such as dust which get everywhere. People allergic to dust need their bedrooms cleaned or dusted regularly.

Medicines called antihistamines can ease some of the symptoms caused by allergies.

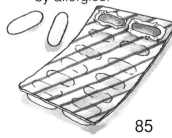

85

How illnesses spread

The most common way that illnesses are spread is through the air. When you cough, sneeze or breathe out, you spray tiny droplets into the air. This can spread illnesses such as colds, flu and chickenpox to other people.

Covering your mouth and nose when you cough or sneeze helps stop germs from spreading. One sneeze can shoot germs over three metres (10 feet).

Touching

Some skin infections, such as cold sores or warts, can be spread from one person to another by touching the infected place.

Try not to share other people's things, such as towels or unwashed dishes and cutlery, if they have an infection.

Food

If you do not take enough care with food, germs can make it bad and cause illness. Bacteria grow on fresh food such as meat and milk if it is kept for too long.

Fresh food should always be washed before cooking or eating.

Food lasts longer if it is kept somewhere cold.

A cover protects food from flies, which can carry bacteria.

Washing hands

Always wash your hands after going to the toilet, and before eating or handling food. Dirty hands can spread germs onto food and cause bad upset tummies.

Soil can occasionally carry a serious disease caused by dog or cat mess, so take care to wash your hands after playing outside in parks or gardens.

Occasionally some pets can pass on diseases. It is always best to wash your hands after handling animals, and not to kiss them, or let them lick your face.

Headlice

Headlice are tiny creatures that can live in your hair and make your head feel itchy. Lice and their eggs (called nits) can get from one person's head to another's.

Tie long hair back for school, and don't share brushes or combs.

Bad water

Water can also carry diseases. This sometimes happens in poorer places where people have to share the same dirty water for washing, drinking and cooking.

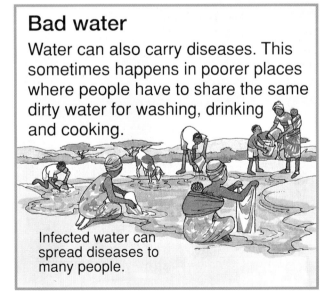

Infected water can spread diseases to many people.

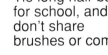

Accidents

If ever you get hurt or injured, whether it is a tiny cut or a broken leg, your body has its own ways of mending itself.

Cuts and grazes

If your skin is broken by a cut or graze and your blood vessels are damaged, blood flows out of your body. Tiny blood cells called platelets soon stop the bleeding by making a sticky plug called a clot.

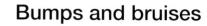

Bumps and bruises

A hard bump can damage blood vessels without breaking your skin. Blood leaks out underneath your skin, but it cannot escape. This causes a bruise.

Chemicals from red blood cells can make bruises look purple.

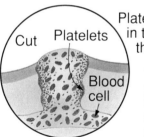

Platelets clump together in the blood around the cut.

Cut   Platelets

Blood cell

The platelets catch other blood cells and make a clot.

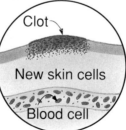

Clot

New skin cells

Blood cell

A bump on a bony part of your body, such as your shin or head, can cause a lump. Your skin swells because there is less room underneath for the blood to drain away.

A blood clot becomes a scab which protects the cut while it heals. Underneath, new skin cells are made to replace the damaged ones. Soon the scab dries up and falls off.

88

Broken bones

If a bone gets broken, your body has to make new cells to grow over the break and join the bone together again. The bone must be set (put) in the right position and kept still while it mends.

Special photographs called X-rays show where and how the bone is broken.

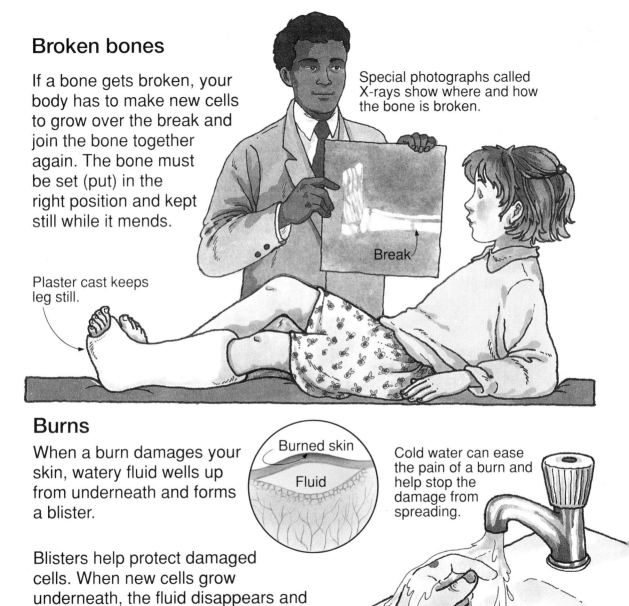

Break

Plaster cast keeps leg still.

Burns

When a burn damages your skin, watery fluid wells up from underneath and forms a blister.

Burned skin

Fluid

Cold water can ease the pain of a burn and help stop the damage from spreading.

Blisters help protect damaged cells. When new cells grow underneath, the fluid disappears and the old, damaged skin peels away.

89

Going to the doctor

Sometimes you may need help from a doctor to get better. A doctor's job is to recognize an illness and try to put things right.

Finding out what's wrong

The doctor asks you questions about how you are feeling. If you can describe your symptoms clearly, it helps her to tell what is wrong. She also looks and feels for any signs of illness such as a rash or swelling.

The doctor may feel your neck. If the lymph nodes there are swollen, it shows you have an infection.

She may put a thermometer under your tongue to take your temperature. It should be about 37°C (98.4°F).

A stethoscope makes sounds inside you louder so she can check that your heart and lungs are working properly.

Records of your health and past visits give the doctor clues to what is wrong.

She uses a special light to look inside your ears, throat and eyes.

When a doctor is working out what is wrong with you, it is called making a diagnosis. Once she has done this, the doctor can then give you advice about getting better.

Hospital

Occasionally your doctor may decide to send you to a hospital. Here you can see another doctor who knows all about your particular illness. In different parts of a hospital doctors treat different illnesses.

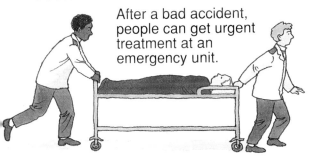

After a bad accident, people can get urgent treatment at an emergency unit.

If you have to stay in a hospital for a while, nurses will look after you. A close member of your family may be able to stay with you and friends can visit to cheer you up.

Medicine

2 spoonfuls twice a day.

Sometimes doctors have to prescribe medicine to help you get better. Medicines must be used just as the doctor says, otherwise they may not work, or could be dangerous.

Doctors on the move

In parts of the world far from towns, people cannot easily get to a doctor so doctors travel to see them. They stay a short while in each place to give people treatment, and advice about staying healthy.

Where you live

People's health is affected by where they live, what they do and how much money they have. Different illnesses are found in different parts of the world.

Weather

The weather can affect people's health. For instance, in hot, wet parts of the world, mosquitoes can spread a serious disease called malaria.

Mosquitoes can infect people with malaria when they bite them.

Food

In some poorer parts of the world, there is not always enough food to go around. Without all the goodness they need from food, people can get very ill. This is called malnutrition.

Red areas on this map show poorer parts of the world.

AFRICA

In parts of Africa, many people die every year from malnutrition.

Not all food is good for you. In richer parts of the world many people suffer from diseases which doctors think may be caused by eating too much of the wrong kind of food.

This meal has lots of sugar and fat, which is bad for you.

Pollution

Pollution can harm all living things, including people. For instance, polluted lakes and rivers can make people ill if the water gets into their drinking supplies.

Overcrowding

Illness can spread quickly in places where people live crowded together without good health care. A disease that infects many people at one time in this way is called an epidemic.

In 1990 an epidemic of cholera in South America affected many people who lived in poor places like the one in this picture.

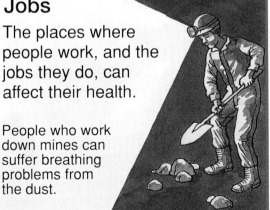

Jobs

The places where people work, and the jobs they do, can affect their health.

People who work down mines can suffer breathing problems from the dust.

Knowing the facts

Learning about how your body works and how illnesses happen helps you live a healthier life.

Years ago nobody knew that smoking caused serious heart and lung diseases. Now people can learn to stay healthier by not smoking.

93

Staying healthy

There are lots of things you can do to help you stay healthy. These are some of them.

Eating well

You need to eat many different types of food to stay really healthy. How much you eat is important too. Eating too much or too little can be unhealthy.

Foods like rice, pasta and potatoes give you energy.

Meat, chicken and fish help you grow.

Dairy products such as cheese make your bones and teeth grow strong.

Fruit and vegetables contain vitamins which keep your body working well.

Keeping yourself clean

Keeping your body clean can help stop germs from causing infections.

Washing and brushing your hair helps keep headlice away.

Brushing your teeth regularly helps prevent tooth decay. Tiny pieces of food that stick in your mouth can produce acids which rot your teeth.

Cleaning your fingernails gets rid of any dirt that might carry germs.

Cuts and grazes should be washed and kept protected.

Washing your hands after going to the toilet or before eating helps stop many germs from spreading.

PASTA

Being careful

You can avoid many accidents and injuries by being careful of things that can harm you.

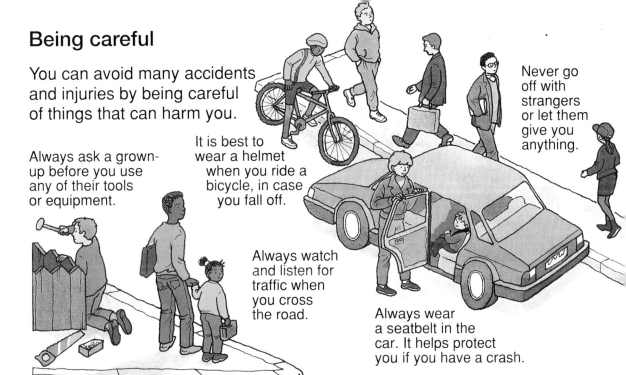

Always ask a grown-up before you use any of their tools or equipment.

It is best to wear a helmet when you ride a bicycle, in case you fall off.

Never go off with strangers or let them give you anything.

Always watch and listen for traffic when you cross the road.

Always wear a seatbelt in the car. It helps protect you if you have a crash.

Exercise

Exercising is a good way of looking after your body. It keeps it in good working order and helps prevent illness.

Swimming is good for people with asthma because it helps improve their breathing.

Feeling good

If ever you feel worried or upset, it can help to talk to somebody you know well and trust. Your friends and family can often make you feel better. Having friends and feeling loved is good for everybody's health.

95

Index

Insect answers

Page 38 - none of the
insects in the picture
is really a wasp.
Number 1 is a fly,
number 2 is a beetle
and number 3 is a
moth.
You can see a real
wasp on page 36.

First published in 1993 by Usborne Publishing Ltd, 83-85 Saffron Hill, London EC1N 8RT, England. Copyright © 1993
Usborne Publishing Ltd. First published in America August 1993.

The name Usborne and the device 🪂 are Trade Marks of Usborne Publishing Ltd. All rights reserved. No part of this
publication may be reproduced, stored in a retrieval system, or transmitted in any form or by any means, electronic,
mechanical, photocopy, recording or otherwise, without the prior permission of the publisher. UE. Printed in Belguim.